The Big Splash!

By Shea Fontana
Illustrated by Erik Doescher

A Random House PICTUREBACK® Book
Random House New York

 Published in the United States by Random House Children's Books, a division of Penguin Random House LLC, 1745 Broadway, New York, NY 10019, and in Canada by Penguin Random House Canada Limited, Toronto. Pictureback, Random House, and the Random House colophon are registered trademarks of Penguin Random House LLC.
rhcbooks.com
dcsuperherogirls.com
dckids.com
ISBN 978-1-5247-6868-3 (trade) — ISBN 978-1-5247-6869-0 (ebook)

Printed in the United States of America

10 9 8 7 6 5 4 3 2 1

"Come on in, Katana! The water's fine," called Bumblebee from Super Hero High School's swimming pool. Katana gulped as she looked down at the deep water. On dry land, Katana was strong, cool, and confident, but being in the water made her nervous. Unfortunately, the swimming test for Coach Wildcat's PE class was tomorrow.

Before the girls could help Katana, the Save the Day Alarm rang. There was trouble at the Metropolis Pier! The heroes raced from Super Hero High to the seaside scene in Katana's high-powered boat.

“That’s not a shark attack. It’s a King Shark attack!” Batgirl said when she saw the ocean-dwelling super-villain rampaging on the pier.

“Poseidon’s Pearls are here somewhere!” snarled King Shark.

Wonder Woman tried to catch King Shark in her Lasso of Truth, but the sleek villain slipped out of her grasp.

"Poseidon's Pearls are part of a magical necklace that doubles the strength of whoever possesses it," Batgirl shouted, checking her communicator. "If King Shark finds it, he could cause even more trouble!"

Lightning-fast, Katana slid behind King Shark just as Bumblebee hit him with her electric beestings. The villain tumbled into the pier's fancy fountain.

"Uber-fierce teamwork!" Katana said, just as King Shark reached up from the fountain and found . . .

“The Pearls!” the villain shouted, grabbing the necklace. “Now I will rule the ocean!”

"We can't let him get back to the sea!" Wonder Woman shouted. The heroes went after the villain as he headed toward the water. Katana's sword and Bumblebee's stings bounced off him, and he snapped Batgirl's Batrope with ease!

“Nice try, but you’re mere minnows compared to my power now,” King Shark taunted the heroes as he dove into the ocean. “If you wanna catch this shark, you’ll have to go fishing!”

“I’ll try to spot him from above,” Wonder Woman said as the other heroes jumped into Katana’s boat.

“How will we find him when the entire surf is his turf?” asked Bumblebee.

“The boat’s sonar can track him . . . ,” Batgirl replied.

“He’s . . . right under us. Watch out!” said Katana.
King Shark took a bite out of the boat and grabbed Wonder Woman from the air. Then he pulled her into the water.

Wonder Woman could hold her breath for a long time, but Batgirl, Bumblebee, and Katana were going to need scuba gear to stay underwater.

"Jumping into the water gives me major butterflies," Katana said nervously. "But there's no way I'm letting tall, dark, and toothy take my friend!"

Katana knew she had to be courageous. She also knew they needed a plan. She told her friends what she had in mind, and they dove into the sea.

“Why do I have to be the bait?” asked Bumblebee as Katana finished setting the trap for King Shark.

“Because you’re the only one who can shrink,” answered Batgirl. “Plus, sharks are attracted to vibrations, like the ones made by your wings.”

"Yum, dessert!" said King Shark when he saw Bumblebee in the cage.

As King Shark entered the cage, Bumblebee shrank and slipped through the bars. Katana swam up behind King Shark and sliced the Pearls from his neck. She slammed the door behind him.

Without the Pearls, King Shark wasn't strong enough to break free. "Hook, line, and sinker," said Katana.

Batgirl swam over to help Wonder Woman get free. The Pearls were secured, but the heroes weren't out of danger yet!

"Uh-oh, looks like my wing vibrations attracted more than just King Shark," said Bumblebee.

"Don't worry. I'll take care of them," said Katana with a smile.

Katana grabbed some starfish and threw them like they were ninja stars, and the sharks fled.

Back on the pier, some of the other heroes had arrived to help clean up the mess made by King Shark. Everyone cheered for the girls who had saved the day.

"Excellent work, students! I'll get these Pearls back where they belong," said Principal Waller. "And I think *someone* has a swimming test to get ready for."

The next day, Katana aced Coach Wildcat's test. She learned that she could be a hero anywhere. Now she was truly fearless—on land *and* in the water!